TIFFANY REISZ'S GODWICKS SERIES

They're rich, titled, and decadent. They appreciate fine art —the more wicked, the better. They're also, quite literally, haunted by sins of the past. They are the Godwicks.

This sampler includes three scenes excerpted from the Godwicks erotic romance and erotic fantasy novels, as well as the full text of "The Beguiling of Merlin," a Godwicks short story that ties into *The Red*.

Standalone Novels — Read in Any Order

The Red ebook is currently an Amazon Kindle exclusive. The print and audiobook versions, however, are available at all retailers.

THE GODWICKS

SAMPLER

TIFFANY REISZ

8TH CIRCLE PRESS • LOUISVILLE, KY

CONTENTS

THE RIDING CROP
EXCERPT FROM "THE RED"

Mona Lisa St. James made a deathbed promise that she would do anything to save her mother's art gallery. Just as she realizes she has no choice but to sell it, a mysterious man offers to save The Red...but only if she agrees to submit to him for the period of one year.

THE
RED

This time Malcolm hadn't marked a page in the big white book of art history. The book on her desk was the most recent auction catalog from London. She turned to the page he'd marked and saw what there was to see...and what there was to see was a late eighteenth-century portrait from English Catholic artist James Sharples.

Portrait of a Gentleman, Small, Three-Quarter Length, Seated on a Chair, In Hunting Attire, A Riding Crop in His Right Hand.

That was certainly it. She saw a dashing gentleman. She saw the canvas was indeed quite small. She saw the man in the portrait was seated on a chair and that he wore hunting attire and in his hand he held a riding crop.

It was a very accurate title for the painting.

So it was to be the crop this time? He'd warned her of that, too. She'd never had a lover beat her before, consensually or otherwise. Her mother had never spanked her. She'd had her bottom pinched by a boy in a bookshop once, and she was ready to slap him when she saw he was no more than fourteen. She'd gotten her revenge by telling on him to his mother, who'd been drinking tea in the café while her son pretended to look at books. The mother had dragged him from the shop by his ear and Mona had smiled all the while. A good memory but not erotic. She didn't imagine she would enjoy being beaten by a riding crop, but who knew? She never thought she'd enjoy frolicking with nymphs or being sold on the auction block or having a bottle stuffed inside her either. And yet she had enjoyed it.

She'd enjoyed it all.

As Malcolm had given her no instructions for what to

wear for their Sunday night assignation, she wore her favorite fall dress of crushed red velvet—ankle length, skin tight, backless. She pinned her apple-red hair up in a chignon and let tendrils fall down her neck. If that wouldn't please a man such as Malcolm, nothing would.

Midnight came at last.

Mona went to the gallery, and spent a moment petting sweet, sleepy Tou-Tou in his bed before heading for the back room. She didn't want to seem afraid, so she opened the door without hesitation.

Malcolm was waiting.

He stood in the center of the back room, his back to her. He'd dressed like the man in the portrait. Hunting attire. White breeches, a green velvet jacket, and brown leather riding boots that clung to his thighs like a second skin. He was magnificent, resplendent, utterly desirable. His hair looked a shade longer and a shade lighter, and it was curled on his head in the consummate Regency style.

In his right hand he held a long wooden riding crop with a leather tip.

Mona ignored the crop. She cared nothing about it. She walked to Malcolm, almost ran, and he took her into his arms and kissed her passionately. His mouth was warm and tasted of spiced wine and cigars. She couldn't stop kissing him.

"Beautiful girl," he murmured against her lips. She wanted to tear off his fine white linen cravat and lick the hollow of his throat. She would have kissed it and bitten it. She would have drunk wine out of it. She hadn't given that hollow a second thought until it was covered and hidden from her view.

"I want you already," she said as she grasped the back

of his coat and pressed her breasts to his chest. He kissed the tops of her breasts, swelling out of her dress. He ran his fingertips over those soft swells and she shivered and sighed. Her nipples needed sucking and her clitoris needed licking and her pussy needed his cock. She was pleased they would be all alone tonight, their first time all alone together in months. She had things she must ask him, but she knew she couldn't until he'd spent his lust on her. It would be hours, she knew, if the pattern held.

She could wait.

Malcolm had looped the leather cord of the riding crop over his right wrist, and she felt the tip of it tickling her backside as he kissed her mouth. He lightly scored her back with his fingertips, caressing her skin along her spine, cupping her bottom before tickling his way up to the nape of her neck again. He kissed her earlobe, kissed her collarbone. As he kissed her neck, he pulled the strap of her dress down her shoulder to bare her left breast. He held it in his hand, squeezed it as he kissed her mouth. He cupped it in his palm and looked down, smiling at it like a prized possession.

"So lovely," he said. "So young and ripe." He teased the tender red tip with his thumb, tracing the edge of the aureole. Her nipple hardened quickly. It was a red marble under the pad of his thumb. He toyed with it to make her moan. "Tell me what you feel, Mona. Tell me what I do to your body."

"I feel desire."

"Tell me much more than that. How does your nipple feel?"

"Hard. It feels as hard to me as it does to you," she said

breathlessly. "A woman can feel when her nipples are this hard."

"As a man can when his cock is hard."

"Yes, I'm sure it's something like that. When you touch my nipple when it's soft, I feel pleasure. But when you touch it when it's this hard, the pleasure is magnified. Ten or twenty times. It's hard to stand, hard to breathe. I ache, Malcolm."

"Where do you ache, Mona? Tell me everywhere you ache." He whispered the order and kissed the top of her breast. His soft hair tickled the bare flesh of her chest. She would die if he made her wait for him to take her.

"My breasts ache," she said. "They need to be licked and sucked hard. And I ache inside for your cock."

"In your cunt."

"In my cunt," she said. He inhaled sharply as if it aroused him to hear her say the word. "It's not just the cunt. The ache is everywhere. In my stomach. In my thighs. Everywhere you touch me. I ache everywhere, Malcolm."

"Here?" he asked and flicked his tongue across her nipple.

"Yes." The word came out in a gasp.

"Here?" He slid his hand into the long slit of her dress at the top of her thigh. He cupped her between her legs, cupped her cunt, and slipped a finger into her wet hole. She contracted around it involuntarily. Malcolm flinched and she knew he'd felt it.

"Yes..." she hissed.

"Here?" He kissed her chest over her heart. "Do you ache for me here?"

"Malcolm…you told me not to love you. Don't make me love you."

"But do you miss me when I'm gone?" he asked.

"The things you do to me…I'd never dare dream them, much less do them. And yet, when I'm with you, there is no game I wouldn't play, nothing of my body would I keep from you. You leave me and I go mad with waiting. You leave me and you are my every waking thought and my every sleeping dream. And if I knew when you were returning to me, I would count the minutes until I saw you again." She paused. "No, that's a lie."

"What's the truth, Mona?" His voice was so soft and tender it hurt her.

"I would count the seconds."

They breathed together, looking into each other's eyes. His mouth closed over hers again and they were locked into a kiss that would seemingly never end.

Then it did.

Malcolm panted. He released her breast and wrapped that arm around her back again, pulling her roughly against him.

"What you feel for me is what I want you to feel tonight," he said. "But you might hate me after."

"I could never hate you."

"Don't say things like that," he warned. "Men like me take statements such as that as a challenge."

"Will you beat me very brutally tonight?"

"I will."

"Will I like it?"

"If you let yourself."

"I'll try," she said, scared but willing. Anything for Malcolm. Especially tonight. She'd never met a man who conformed so closely to her ideal. She felt the smooth leather of his riding boot against her bare calf. She rubbed her leg against it like a cat rubbing its cheek against a chair leg it wanted to mark. She ran her hands down the velvet of his broad back, cupped his firm backside and held it while he kissed her. Of their own accord her hips pushed into his again and again. Her sex was already open for him, wet and slick, hollowed out and waiting. If he put his cock into her right now, she'd come before he'd even bottomed out inside her on the first stroke.

But he didn't take her.

"Listen to me, Mona." He put his hands on her neck, lightly cupping it, his thumbs pressing into the hollow of her throat to force her to pay attention to his words. She dropped her hands to her sides and met his dark flinty eyes again. "You'll be mine tonight in a way you've never been mine before. It's one thing to allow a man to pleasure you. It's quite another to allow him to hurt you. You'll know real powerlessness tonight, real fear, true pain. And I will drink it like wine."

"You like my pain?"

"I love your submission to pain. It's human nature to race toward pleasure and flee from pain. That you would fight your own nature to please me by suffering my crop arouses me more than anything you've done for me before."

"I want to please you." She placed her hands on his trim waist, feeling the heavy brocade cloth of his vest and the heat of his body under her hands. "After all, that's what you're paying me for."

"Oh…you will be beaten for that." He eyes narrowed and she saw he meant it.

"Good," she said. "If I'm going to be beaten, I want to have earned it."

"You earned it when you crossed the threshold. You earned it when you sold your body to me." He stepped back from her, putting breathing room between them. She already felt cool without the heat of his body against hers. "Show me my property. Show me what I got for my money."

Mona slipped the other strap of her gown off her shoulder and lowered the bodice. She gathered the fabric in her hands at her waist and pushed it all the way to her ankles. Naked but for the red high heeled shoes she wore, she stepped out of the dress and onto the floor.

"A blank canvas," Malcolm said as he walked a circuit around her naked body. "I'll enjoy painting you red and blue."

She quaked in her shoes with fear and arousal. She'd never been with a man as beautiful as Malcolm and she would have walked barefoot across a pit of red coals to please him tonight...but he was right. Reason called to her, telling her to run from the pain.

She ignored its voice. It sounded too much like her own. She'd far rather listen to Malcolm's.

"Put your arms behind your head," he said. "Clasp your fingers and keep your elbows open. Like a butterfly's wings."

She did as she was told. The move made her arch her back, thrust her breasts forward. Malcolm stood before her, inspecting her.

"Legs wider," he said. He touched the floor with the tip of the riding crop in two places—here and there, showing her where to place her feet. She moved her feet wider apart, a foot and a half, and stood quivering in place.

"Very nice." Malcolm raised the crop and tapped her left nipple with it. Then her right. He caressed the underside of each breast with the triangle of leather on the crop's end. He ran the shaft of the crop down the sides of her body from each elbow to each ankle and back up again. It tickled and made her shiver. She would have given anything to feel Malcolm's body against her right now. She craved it and with every passing second she craved it more. No doubt this was the intention.

He stepped close again. It was torture to be so close without touching. He brought the crop up between them and pressed the flat side of the tip to his lips. Then he pressed the opposite side to her lips.

"Think of it as a kiss," he said when the leather lay against her mouth. "That's all it is. Just a kiss from me to you."

"Most kisses don't leave welts," she said. "I prefer French kissing."

"Well, I'm English. This is English kissing."

Then stepping back again, he brought the crop's leather tip between her legs and lightly tapped her sex. He turned it on its side and used the edge of the tip to pry her apart along the seam of her vulva. She felt the stiff leather corner against the entrance of her body.

"It stings more if it's wet," he said with his devil's grin and for a split second she wondered…what if Malcolm was the devil? With a riding crop in her cunt, she could almost believe it.

So what if he was? She wanted him all the same.

He dipped the riding crop's tip into her sex again, wetting it with her own fluids.

"Insult to injury," she said.

He held his arms wide, smiled, and bowed. "The name of the game, my darling."

She nodded her acquiescence.

"Here are the rules," he said. "You survive my crop, you earn my cock. A hundred strikes of this." He lifted the crop into the air. "For a hundred strokes of this." He pointed casually at his crotch and she could see the outline of his erection through the pale breeches. The trousers adhered so tightly to his body she could even see one long vein running from the base along to the shaft to the tip. She knew that vein. She'd licked it with her own tongue.

A hundred strokes of his cock? She'd come after the first ten, if not on the very first.

"Count for me," he said. "Starting at a hundred."

He stood behind her and she braced herself. What was he waiting for? Was he torturing her with suspense? Taking his aim?

"Admiring the view," he said as if reading her thoughts. She blushed hot at the flattery and smiled. Then he wiped the smile off her face with one quick crack of the crop. It struck high on her thigh in a spot she'd never associated with agony before. It burned like Greek fire.

She cried out in shock and Malcolm laughed.

The bastard *laughed* at her.

"Count, dear," he said, his voice chiding.

"One hundred."

"Did it hurt?" he asked, tenderly touching the burning welt on her thigh.

"Yes," she said.

"I'm sorry, darling." He kissed his fingertips and touched them to the welt. "So very sorry."

Then he kissed her lips softly and massaged her nipples. She moaned in the back of her throat. Her body was a carnival of sensations—the stinging pain, the swelling of her breasts, the tingling of her lips as he kissed her. Her head spun. Did he want to hurt her? If so, then why apologize and kiss her to make up for it?

"There we go, love," he said. "Only ninety-nine to go. Don't feel too bad. When I was fifteen, I was caught buggering my neighbor's lady wife. I would have traded my left ball for a punishment like this."

"Were you beaten?"

"I was."

"With a crop?"

"A bullwhip."

She gasped.

"Like I said, it could be worse. So count your blessings when you count my kisses."

He struck her again with the crop, kissing her hip this time.

"Ninety-nine," she said through the pain.

"Such a good girl," Malcolm said, hitting the side of her neck over the pulse point. "Beautiful and brave. You can't know how much you please me…"

He struck her again, out of nowhere, right on the back of the calf. Her leg almost buckled from the shock and the pain.

"Malcolm—"

"It's all right…" He put his arm around her to hold her up. He cupped her chin in his hand, tilted her face up to his and kissed the tip of her nose. "It's not so bad, is it?"

"No," she said. In his arms, it wasn't so bad. It wasn't so bad at all.

He struck her again. Mona closed her eyes as the pain washed through her. It wasn't unbearable, but it wasn't pleasant either. After a few dozen strikes, it might very well become unbearable, however.

Yet nothing would allow her to break before she'd earned what she wanted and what she wanted was him.

He walked around her body, striking her with the crop high and low—on her thighs, on her stomach, on her breasts, on her backside, so often and so hard she knew she'd hardly be able to sit in a chair tomorrow. But what did tomorrow mean to her when she wasn't certain she'd survive tonight?

The crop didn't sting like a bee. It bit like a snake. Its fangs were sharp and burning and left sharp and burning bite marks all over her body. Malcolm was the snake-charmer and she was mesmerized by how he made the crop dance. He would twirl it in his fingers, casual, playful. Then he'd catch it quick, so fast she couldn't see where the blow would come from and where it would land.

It would have been easier for her to close her eyes tight and pretend it wasn't happening, wait it out, hide inside her mind. But she couldn't. Malcolm wouldn't allow that. After each strike he paused to kiss her, to fondle her breasts and nipples, to massage her hips and quivering belly. After each strike he'd tell her how beautiful she was. He'd tell her what a brave, brave girl she was. He'd tell her how aroused she made him with her submission to his crop. He'd kiss her on the mouth, before suddenly stepping back to strike her once more. Then the cycle would begin again. The crop, the pain, the tender words and tender kisses. Soon she was craving the crop because each strike meant a kiss.

Before he'd begun, a hundred hits sounded like a hundred too many. But each strike earned such affection from Malcolm, such compassion, such sympathy that she was starting to think one hundred wasn't nearly enough. He was forcing her to fall in love—not with him, but with the crop.

She was in love with the crop. The crop, and Malcolm's tender sadism.

And Malcolm too, of course. How could she not? He was inhumanly attractive. His eyes were so black and the room so dark she couldn't tell the iris apart from the pupil. As he shifted this way and that to keep her guessing, the muscles in his thighs tensed and shone through his breeches. His boots sported gold buttons at the tops and she wanted to kiss them for some reason. The thought wouldn't leave her head. She trained her eyes on them, on the glinting gold coins, and let them anchor her into the moment.

"You're staring at my boots, love. Tell me why," he said. He took her in his arms and held her close against him. The crop dangled from his wrist as he ran the flat of his hand down her brutalized back.

"I like them." She panted between the words. Pain suffused her body. Her flesh smoldered like a hot sidewalk in the rain.

"I'm very glad you do. What do you like about them?"

"The gold buttons," she said. "I can't stop looking at them."

"I'll tell you what, my darling girl," he said. "If you can take ten strikes in a row without me stopping, I'll let you kiss those buttons on my boots. What do you think? Would you like that?"

"Very much," she said.

"What do you say to me?"

"Thank you, Malcolm."

"That's very nice, yes. Could you call me sir? I think I'd like to hear it from you. Everything you say sounds so pretty."

"I'll say anything you want, sir."

"Oh, that is even better than I thought it would be. Excellent. You've made me so very happy tonight." He pressed a soft kiss to her lips once more. She would never tire of his kisses or his words of affection or his pride in her. How had she ever lived without this in her life? Without the crop and the counting and the pain that earned her such rewards, would she have eagerly signed up for a thousand strikes of the crop for the next thousand years?

"Are you ready, dear? Only ten. I know you can do it. I know you will do it—for me, won't you?"

"Of course, sir," she said, and her heart welled and she could have wept with love for him. What wouldn't she do for him? Nothing. The answer was nothing. She would take his English kisses over French kisses any day.

She took a breath in and braced herself. Her hands were still on her head. Her arms ached but she didn't care.

When the strike came she was ready. It hit her on an unmarked patch of flesh on the side of her hip. The second strike came right after, in the very same spot. And the third. And the fourth. It was agony by the fifth, terrible agony by the sixth, screaming agony by the seventh. And the eighth and the ninth and the tenth passed in a haze as she wept and shook.

Malcolm caught her in his arms again as she swayed on her feet. "I've got you," he said. "You're safe. You're with me."

She rested her head on his shoulder as he stroked her hair. She put her arms around his neck and he let her.

"I know that hurt, didn't it?" he asked and she nodded. "I'm sorry. You're doing so well though."

"It hurts so much," she said. "I didn't know it could hurt that much."

"You're taking it like you were born for the crop. I wish I had a hundred men here to watch and see what a prize you are. I wouldn't sell you to the highest bidder, not for all the money in the world."

She needed to hear that. It was a balm to her soul. "Thank you, sir," she said.

"Here," he said. "This might help a little."

He put the crop's strap around his wrist again and slipped his hand between her legs. He stroked her labia and clitoris while she clung to his shoulders to steady herself.

"Isn't that nice, love?" he asked.

She nodded against his shoulder, looking down to watch him touch her. She was hot between her legs, hot inside. When he stuck a finger up and into her, she gave a little cry of pleasure.

"That's my girl." He spoke to her like she was a child in need of soothing. So caring. So kind. It was easy to forget that he wasn't simply the solace for her suffering, he was the cause of it. And she loved the suffering as much as the solace. What had he done to her?

"Can I come, sir?" She wanted to climax very badly. She could take more pain, if only she could come. Already his fingers were bringing her close. And his hands were so well-proportioned and muscular and lovely that she could rest her head on his shoulder and watch him touch her sex all night and all day.

"Can you come?" He chuckled lightly even as he wiggled his finger inside her. "What sort of question is that? No. Not yet. You know it's not time yet, silly girl."

"I'm sorry, sir."

"It's fine. It's fine," he said soothingly. "I know it's hard, but you're doing so well. I would hate for you to give up already."

"I won't give up."

"That's the spirit." He grinned at her and tickled her inside to make her laugh. "Now I believe you've earned a treat. Haven't you?"

"If you say I have."

"And I say you have." He stopped touching her, but that was for the best. She was almost ready to orgasm. If she did, she knew she'd be in terrible trouble. Even worse, she would have disappointed him, and she couldn't live with herself if she disappointed him. Not that. Anything but that.

She slowly sank down to the floor, using his body—so solid and sturdy—to steady herself. Once on her knees, it was near torture not to unfasten the falls of his breeches and take his cock into her mouth and suck it. But that wasn't what she was here for, even though he was stiff and straining so hard against the white fabric she saw it throbbing. She rested her head for a moment against his rock hard thigh and sighed with indescribable pleasure when Malcolm caressed her hair.

"My Mona," he said. "My darling."

She touched the side of his calf and stroked the leather of his boot from his ankle to his knee. It was smooth and supple and she couldn't get enough of it. The two gold coin buttons glinted in the candlelight. First she kissed her fingertips and pressed the kiss to the buttons. Then she brought her lips down to them and kissed them with her mouth. Malcolm shuddered. She felt it go through his body and into hers. She kissed his boots again, kissed the gold buttons, kissed the leg of the boot that was warm from the heat of his body. While she was on the floor on her hands and knees, Malcolm caressed her sex again with the tip of the crop. She spread her legs wider for him and arched her back, offering her cunt up to him.

He struck it with the crop.

She screamed in sudden agony even though she knew he would do it, even though she wanted him to do it.

"Count, love," he said. "You know you have to count."

"Forty-nine," she said. She'd survived fifty-one strikes already and that last one was worse than all of them combined.

"We're over halfway there," he said as she rested her head against his thigh again. "You've made it so far and so well. Are you tired?"

She nodded and whispered, "Yes, sir."

"I know you're tired." He reached down and lightly brushed her lips with his fingers, lightly teased her cheek with a lock of her own hair. That made her smile. "There's my girl. So obedient. She's even smiling."

"Why do you do this?" she asked, so torn between loving the crop and hating it, loving him and hating him. "Why, sir?"

"I do it out of kindness, of course," he said. "You understand that, don't you?"

She thought of his kisses, his sweet words, and the caring way he touched her welts. He was a kind man. Who but a kind man would give her such affection, such tender concern with her pain?

"I understand, sir. You are very kind." It made her smile to say it, not because it was a lie but because it was true. She understood it all now.

"Now only forty-eight more. Do you want to take them on the floor or would you like to stand again?"

A choice. How kind of him.

"The floor, please, sir."

"If you like," he said. "On your hands and knees. You'll be more comfortable that way. Legs wide. There. Just lovely. I love to see you like this," he said, standing behind her. She knew he was looking at her open and exposed holes. She wanted him to see them. She wanted him to see what he owned. "I'm so very glad I asked you to play this game with me."

"It's my pleasure, sir."

"Oh, I know it is, but it's so rare to find such an eager partner. In truth, my dear, you're really doing me a favor."

She looked up and he had his hands on his chest. So well-mannered. So refined. So civilized. The very portrait of a gentleman indeed.

He took the crop in hand and struck her under her ribcage so hard she went momentarily blind.

He was an angel of beauty and pain.

"Count, darling," he said. "Otherwise I'll forget my place and we'll have to start all over. I hate losing my place, don't you?"

He was the devil incarnate.

"Forty-eight," she said through gritted teeth.

"That's right. Almost there. Carry on. That's my girl."

Angel.

"Oh, that hurt my hand so I know it must have hurt you. I'm so sorry, my darling."

Demon.

On and on it went. The hits followed by words of encouragement and affection followed by more hits. Mona grew dizzy. It was hard to keep count but unthinkable to lose count. What if he started over? What if he didn't? Even as she counted, it seemed time had stopped. The clock stopped. The world stopped. They had always played this game and they always would. That was how it should be. Heaven and hell were in this room and they had one foot in each.

"Only ten left, sweetheart. You're amazing, you know. Simply amazing at this."

She counted the last few strikes and by the final five she'd curled into the fetal position on the hardwood floor. Two left. Just two.

"Darling?" Malcolm's voice penetrated the fog of her suffering. "My angel girl?"

"Yes, sir?"

"You need to lie on your back for me. All right?"

She whimpered in pain as she unfurled herself from

the self-protective cocoon she'd rolled herself into. Every movement left her body in misery. She felt like an old book that hadn't been opened in centuries and now someone had come at last, taken the book from the shelf, broken the spine and riffled through pages that had been pressed together so long their ink had turned to glue. Sinews screamed. Muscles moaned. Simply lying on her back had made her weep again. Hot tears poured from her eyes, stealing her peripheral vision, though Malcolm remained in perfect focus. He straddled her at her hips with those boots of his she worshiped, one leather ankle pressed against each side of her body.

"Perfect," he said. He looked her up and down, one hand on his chin and the other on his hip the way he had been the first night she'd seen him. He perused her like the work of an old master. "Wait, not quite. Put your hands behind your head again. I want you to cradle your head. The floor's so hard, I would never want you to hurt yourself."

She loved him for his concern. Had she ever met a man more thoughtful? She placed her hands behind her head and cradled her head in her palms.

"Marvelous." He smiled down at her. "Now two more to go. We can do this together. Ready, my sweet?"

"Ready, sir."

"I haven't the words to tell you how much I've enjoyed this," he said. "I simply don't have the words."

He raised the crop and lashed it down, striking her right breast so hard she screamed, so hard she heard the swish of it in the wind like the sound of a whip.

She coughed from the pain and it was the greatest test of her willpower to choke out the number.

"Two," she said, more tears burning her cheeks.

"Last one, darling. Then we're all done. And won't that be lovely?"

He lashed her again, one final time, striking the side of her left breast. She cried out the last number of her torment and rolled again onto her side, burying her face in her hands to weep.

Far away she heard movement—the rustle of fabric, boot heels on the hardwood. When she'd worn herself out with weeping, she continued to lay there, spent from her suffering and yet strangely peaceful. Though it was all over, the memory of the words Malcolm had said to her during her beating rang in her ears like the chiming of a golden bell.

You're the bravest girl in the world.

My princess, my angel, my darling, my dear.

You're lovelier like this than I've ever seen you.

You can't know what this means to me, what a gift you've given me tonight.

You please me beyond words, Mona.

She heard those words in her ear again, because Malcolm spoke them again. He had come to the floor and taken her in his arms. He lifted her up, holding her like a babe in arms, all the while whispering his admiration of her, his adoration. She put her arms around his strong shoulders and held him as he carried her to the bed. The velvet of his coat prickled against her savaged skin, yet she relished the sensation since it meant he was holding her.

"Here we go," he said, laying her on the bed. He'd pulled the covers back so she lay on the soft white sheet.

For all its softness, she still winced as her sore body met the mattress.

"I know it hurts." Malcolm sat on the bed by her side and took her hand in his. He kissed her wrist, kissed her palm, and all five fingers received their own kisses. Her knuckles too. "I'm so proud of you, dearest."

"Did I please you?"

"More than I can ever say."

He kissed her forehead, kissed her eyelids, kissed her lips.

"Stay there," he said. "I'll tend to your wounds."

"Will you make love to me?"

He smiled, laughed softly. "All night long," he said. "But first I must take care of you. Your well-being is more important than anything else. You know that, don't you?"

These didn't sound like lines from the play they were acting out. Important to him? How? Why? She was his whore. That was all, wasn't it?

"Am I important to you?" she asked.

He brought her hand to his lips again, pressed it to his mouth, and closed his eyes.

"I have waited a very long time for you," he said. "And tonight you've proven to me just how very special you are." He put her hand onto her chest and kissed the back of it. "Rest here. You've earned it."

Mona feared to look at her own body, but she did so anyway. She wanted to see what Malcolm saw. Upon lifting her head, she winced. In stripes along her thighs, and in patches on her stomach, and in whorls on her arms and breasts, she saw deep red welts. Some were pure scarlet red. Others a rusty red with black or blue cores.

She imagined her entire backside from her neck to her knees looked about the same.

She wasn't horrified by what she saw. In truth, she found the welts erotic, because Malcolm had trained her eyes to see kisses where others would see wounds.

Malcolm set the wooden chair next to the bed and on the seat of the chair he placed a bowl of water.

"Only water," he said. "Warm water, not hot. Lie still for me."

She nodded and laid her head back on the pillow. For him. He'd said to lie still for him and for him she would lie still. For him she would move. For him she would live and breathe. For him.

He brought his hands to his throat and unfastened the white linen cravat. He unwound it from his neck and at last there it was, the hollow of his throat, the hollow she'd craved to kiss and lick and worship. She smiled, happier than she'd been in years. He folded the linen into a thick square and dipped it into the bowl of water. Then he wrung it out, flattened it out, and pressed it against one of the screaming red and black welts on her hips. She hissed through her teeth. But soon the pain dissipated and the warmth permeated her skin and sunk into the deep layers of tissue, soothing her down to the bone.

"Better?" Malcolm asked. She gave him a tired smile. He dipped the linen into the water again, pressed it to another welt where it quieted the screaming of her skin. For a long time, he ministered to her wounds. Not a single one was missed. When he finished with the front of her body, she rolled onto her stomach and rested her cheek against the pillow. He'd asked her if she knew how important she was to him. No, she didn't know. But she felt it. The way he tended to her welts, to her needs, with such solicitude was beyond anything she'd experienced from a lover before. She felt spoiled as an only child, treasured as a prized possession, doted on like a king's most favored concubine. What magic was it, what sorcery that could turn an act of violence and pain into an act of adoration and affection? It was alchemy, the art of turning base things into gold.

"Would you give me permission to love you, sir?" she asked Malcolm.

"You may tonight," he said, the slightest smile on his lips to show how secretly pleased he was. "You won't love me next time I come to you, so enjoy it while you can."

She laughed softly into the pillow. Hard to take such a threat seriously from a man who was using his own linen cravat to tend to her wounds.

"I don't believe that," she said.

"What did I warn you about saying things like that?"

"I know, I know, sir. Men like you take it as a challenge."

"You only love me tonight because of the beating. You understand that, don't you?"

Before tonight, she would have said "no," that made no sense, there was no logic to it. He'd done something to her mind as well as to her body. By the end of her beating, she couldn't tell the crop apart from his kindnesses. They were one and the same to her so that every strike of the crop was tender as a kiss and every word of tenderness made her crave the crop.

"Now I understand," she said, because now she did.

When he'd finished with the water, he brought out a clear glass bottle of golden oil. It smelled like crushed wildflowers and warmed her skin even more as he rubbed it into her sore flesh. He massaged her entire body—back and legs, shoulders and arms—then bade her roll onto her back again so he could do the same to her front. He lingered long over her breasts, using both of his hands on each one. She gave herself up to his hands, let him mold her like clay. She had no will over her own body. She willed only that Malcolm's will be done.

Malcolm slicked the warm oil all over her stomach and hips and thighs. He brought his hand between her legs and nudged her thighs open. He glazed her clitoris with the oil and stroked circles all around it. It swelled under his touch and pulsed against his finger. She felt that deep delicious hollowness inside her again. He filled it with his fingers when he slid them up into her sex, the oil allowing him deep penetration. It was bliss to spread her legs far apart for him so that he could have his way with her. She watched as his fingers disappeared inside her body one by one, probing and parting her from within. Mona panted through her nose. She knew she mustn't come until his cock was inside her. If he didn't put it there soon she'd be forced to beg him for it.

"Do you have children?" she asked.

He laughed softly. "I have four fingers in your cunt and you're asking me if I have children. Do you think I'm checking to see if there's room for one more?"

She grinned broadly, too tired and aroused to laugh.

"I only wondered," she said.

"Does it matter to you?" he asked.

"I'm nosy. And you're a mystery."

"I have children, yes. Though not so young anymore."

"Do you love them?"

"I love them though they've disappointed me."

"How so?"

"They're…respectable," he said. "Respectable and well-behaved. Good citizens of the realm. They're boring. Except the youngest. He takes after me." His words made her grin drunkenly. "Are you happy to know that?"

"I am," she said. "Although…I don't know why."

"You're open," he said.

"I know I am."

"Not like that though…" He glanced down at his hand that was in her cunt up to the thumb. "I broke you open tonight. Up here." With his free hand he tapped his temple, indicating his mind. "And here." He tapped his chest over his heart. "You feel close to me."

"I do," she said.

"It's the intimacy of captor and captive. There's nothing like it."

"Am I your captive?"

"You are tonight."

"Can you keep me forever?"

"I wish I could," he said, and she believed he meant it. At least tonight he meant it.

"But you can't?"

He shook his head. "But…if you want, you can keep me."

"What does that mean?"

His smile turned him back into that handsome devil she knew and loved.

"You'll see," he said. "Now close your eyes and keep them closed."

She didn't want to obey this order; it was too enjoyable to look at him. But she couldn't refuse him. Mona closed her eyes and relaxed into the soft sheets. She heard the brass headboard rattle as Malcolm slid his body on top of hers. She sensed movement but kept her eyes closed even as she felt him crawling up the bed, over her. First he removed her pillow and laid her flat on her back on the bed. He then lifted her arms and put them over her head. Her arms were slack, her entire body loose and yielding. He was twining the linen cravat around her wrists, securing her to the brass slats of the headboard. Never before had she engaged in bondage with a lover. She should have guessed Malcolm would be her first. She heard fabric rip as Malcolm moved off of her and to her ankles where he used the other half of the cravat to tie each of them to the slats of the footboard. Nothing about being restrained by him scared her. Quite the opposite, she felt swaddled and secure. It was restful to be tied spread-eagle to the bed. She was absolved of all responsibility, absolved of all sin. What could she do? Nothing. She could only lie there passively as he did whatever it was he wanted to do to her. And whatever he wanted to do with her was what she wanted done.

Malcolm crawled over her again. She felt the naked tip of his cock graze her stomach. Her vagina contracted in hungry need for it. But he didn't move down and push it inside her like she wanted. He straddled her head instead.

"Open your eyes," he said, and when she did it was to find him holding the dripping tip at her chin. He didn't have to tell her to take it into her mouth. He placed his hand under the back of her head and lifted it with all the gentleness of a nurse raising the head of a sick patient to drink some water. She did it willingly, wrapping the tip with her lips and sucking. A small burst of semen shot into her mouth and she swallowed it eagerly. It was merely a taste of what was to come. He'd been erect for well over an hour now. Surely he was as ready to orgasm as she was. He slowly fucked her mouth. The only thing more erotic than the taste of him on her tongue was the feel of his leather boots against the sides of her breasts. As much as she relished his naked body, she was pleased he'd kept his clothes on, baring only the organ he needed to fuck her. He was resplendent, and she wanted to know what it was like to be ridden by a man who wore boots for the job in question. God, he had turned her into a whore, hadn't he? A whore with no shame in her whoring, that's what he'd made her. He'd cracked open something in her, some dormant, latent proclivity for pain and punishment and being treated like a possession. She could never go back to the way it was before. Whatever it would take to keep him in her life, she would do it. This devil, this angel, this man. She almost wanted him to make her pregnant. It would be a tie to him, a tether. She pushed the thought from her mind. These were dangerous dreams. What had he done to her?

At this angle she couldn't do much more than lick and suck the tip, but she gave it the full measure of her attention and adoration. She worshiped the organ in her mouth. She served it and its needs, its desires, its wants and thanked it that what it wanted tonight was her.

Malcolm had one hand on his cock as he guided it in and out of her mouth, one hand atop the brass headboard. She loved to hear his ragged breaths. He sounded like he was close to his breaking point. She craved his semen, wanted it inside her—any hole would do. But he kept fucking her mouth, not coming, torturing himself with pleasure as much as he'd tortured her.

Mona sucked it as deep as she could, pulling on it with her mouth, and Malcolm let out a groan of abject ecstasy.

"Fuck…" he breathed and Mona would have smiled if her mouth wasn't otherwise occupied.

Malcolm slowly eased himself from her mouth and moved down her body until his knees straddled her hips.

"Wicked girl," he said. "You almost made me spill all over your face."

"Oh no," she said. "Anything but that."

"You modern girls are so hard to scandalize."

"Is that what you're trying to do?" she asked. "Scandalize me?"

"Is it working?"

"You've turned me into a whore and made me happy about it. Consider me thoroughly scandalized."

He chuckled and it was a sinister mad scientist sound. "If you think you're scandalized now…wait until I'm done with you."

She said nothing to that because she never wanted him to be done with her.

Malcolm lowered his head to her right breast and suckled lightly. She closed her eyes and rested her head back, basking in the bliss of his mouth and the pull and tug on her nipple. It sent rings of heat and pleasure radiating through her chest and stomach, making her inner muscles clench again and again. Her entire sex dampened and stirred, eager for him to enter her. He seemed in no hurry to take her, so she laid there helpless to do anything but enjoy herself. His mouth moved to her other nipple. It hardened as he lapped at it. The aching of the welts had quieted. Before they had screamed at her, but now they merely whispered reminders they were there. The wounds made her very aware of her body. Whenever Malcolm touched one of her welts or bruises, on purpose or by accident, she remembered the kiss of his crop, those words that had melted her down and recast her into a new image. She remembered his twin gifts of pain and tenderness, and she loved him for both.

Without a word of warning, Malcolm lowered his hips and pressed every inch of him into her. She heard herself make a sound, a long low moan, as he filled her to her innermost parts. He rose up and took her breasts in his hands, and he rode her with deep strokes. She couldn't move her legs or her arms, only her hips, which she lifted to meet his thrusts. She heard the wet sounds of their copulating and it aroused her even more. Malcolm seemed lost inside her. His hands held her breasts in a firm grip and his head was back, his lips parted, his eyes closed as he fucked her. He was a god to her now, a god of sex and sin. If he could have fucked her forever, she would let him. In hell where the sins of lust were punished, they said the lascivious damned tore each other apart with their desires, and the rent and bleeding pieces still found ways to meet and mate with each other. How was that hell, she wondered? These theologians had never met Malcolm.

The frenzy gripped her, gripped her around the hips and waist. She needed release and it was driving her mad not to have it. Mona rocked her hips faster, lifted and lifted them.

"Easy, love," Malcolm said, but it was too late. She was past all reason. Wild, she bucked as best as she could beneath him with her ankles and wrists bound to the bed. She bucked and writhed, writhed and begged. But Malcolm held back, fucking her with restraint, as if striking her a hundred times with a riding crop wasn't enough torture for her. Not near enough.

This was the worst torture of them all. She had to come. She had to. No question, no hope, no surrender. She needed him to slam his cock into her a thousand times, but he could not be persuaded. He made her suffering even worse when he plucked at her nipples again. He pinched one, then the other, then back and forth. He was giving her gentle foreplay, when what her sex needed was brutal pounding.

"Are you forgetting something?" he asked. That smile again, that evil devil's grin.

She'd forgotten to count.

One hundred strikes. One hundred strokes. She'd forgotten she was supposed to count his thrusts the ways she'd counted the cropping.

"One hundred," she said when Malcolm thrust into her the very next time.

"Now she remembers," he said, still smiling.

He thrust again, harder, and she contracted inside painfully.

"Ninety-nine."

Malcolm pumped his hips again. These were vicious, sharp thrusts, as punishing as they were pleasurable. She could barely recognize her own voice as she counted them. Ninety-eight, ninety-seven...

"By the way, darling, if you come before one hundred, you'll see a side of me you won't like very much."

Ninety-one. Ninety.

The counting kept her from climaxing. She couldn't do both at the same time. The pressure built. The muscles all along the backs of her thighs were so taut she thought they'd snap any moment. And still she lifted her hips into each thrust, not merely receiving his prick but grasping for it with her sex, taking it as it took her.

Eighty-one. Eighty.

To make it even more miserable, Malcolm continued fondling her breasts, pinching her nipples with each number she called out. Her breasts were so swollen from his attentions, they felt twice their normal size.

Seventy-one. Seventy.

She would have given anything to have her ankles free so she could move her legs. She wanted to spread more for him so he could pound her right into the base of her stomach. The very thought of it made her inner muscles twitch.

Sixty-one. Sixty.

Her throat hurt from breathing so hard. She could still taste the salt of his sperm in her mouth.

Fifty-one. Fifty.

Mona pulled on the bonds that held her wrists fast to the bed, anything to relieve some of the excruciating tension in her body. But nothing helped. She was wound tighter than a clock.

Forty-one. Forty.

Malcolm was fucking her harder now. She knew he had to be as desperate to come as she was. Her breasts bounced as he pumped into her cunt.

Thirty-one. Thirty.

He slapped her breasts lightly, reigniting the red pain

of the welts. A sound briefly interrupted the counting, part scream and part sob.

Twenty-one. Twenty.

She couldn't take anymore. It was too much. Her head swam and her eyes saw nothing even when open. Her sex throbbed and she could barely speak or breathe or move.

Eleven. Ten.

At last he gave her the thrusts she needed. Full body thrusts. The soft linen of his shirt grazed her nipples. The stiff shaft grazed her painfully swollen clitoris. She didn't speak the numbers anymore, she gasped them. The bed rocked underneath her and Malcolm was all over her, sucking her and licking her and biting her and fucking and fucking and fucking her.

Two.

One.

The dam burst inside her. With a cry that surely someone heard out on the streets, she came at last, heels dug into the mattress, hips off the bed, and her sex clenching and clutching wildly all around Malcolm's cock. He was coming into her, spurts and spurts of semen glazing her inner walls. Her entire body shuddered and spasmed as she was overwhelmed with the paroxysms of her climax. It went on forever, forever, and even longer than forever...

Then it was done.

Malcolm lay atop her, barely moving, though she felt a few last gasps of fluid spurting inside her. She was spent. She had never been more spent. He'd taken everything out of her. She had nothing left—no mind, no will, no energy.

"Was that enough for you?" Malcolm asked as he nuzzled her ear, kissed her neck.

Already her sex stirred back to life at the sensual tone of his voice, the kisses, the bite of his teeth on her ear.

"No," she said.

"More?"

"More," she begged. "More and more and more." He started to move again, to fuck her again, to fill her again and with each stroke she said that word. More. It was her only want. Her only need.

More.

And more was exactly what he gave her.

———

THE STORY CONTINUES in The Red, *available now in trade paperback, ebook, library hardcover, and audio from 8th Circle Press and Tantor Audio.*

BRANDED

EXCERPT FROM "THE ROSE"

On the day of Lia Godwick's university graduation party, she receives a beautiful wine cup, a rare artifact known as the Rose kylix. It was used in the temple ceremonies of Eros, Greek god of erotic love, and has the power to bring the most intimate sexual fantasies to life...

THE
ROSE

ugust said nothing as he stepped forward and stood in front of her, naked and lovely and waiting.

She still sat on her leather club chair. Shaking and nervous, she lifted her eyes to his and found he was looking down at her with love. Love? Yes, she couldn't call it anything else. The tenderness in eyes, the kindness, the desire...it looked like she'd always imagined love would look in a man's eyes.

No wonder he made a fortune doing this.

He reached out and stroked her burning face with his fingertips.

"Touch me," he said.

"God," she said, heaving a breath. "Where?"

"Anywhere. Touch me anywhere and any way you like."

He was fully aroused. His cock was thick and red and inches from her face. Lia did want to touch him. She absolutely did. She wanted to touch every inch of him and she knew exactly which inch she wanted to start with...

"Please, Lia," August said softly.

She heard true need in his voice. Well, if he wanted her to...

Lia shook a little in her chair. She was so close to him she could feel the heat emanating from his body. His fingers were still stroking her cheek. She glanced up at him again and saw him watching her, waiting, eager for her to make the first move, to break the tension, to open Pandora's box and see what flew out...

Lia leaned forward and pressed her fingertips against the three-petal rose tattoo. They were thick lines, deep, like scars, not like ink. Like burns. Like a...

With a gasp, she pulled her head back and met his eyes.

"It's a brand," she said.

He nodded.

"Did it hurt?"

"Have you ever been branded? Of course it hurt."

"I'm sorry."

"I'm not. I was branded after I was with my first patron," August said. "First time in my life I felt truly alive, truly…human."

She touched the brand again, as gently as she could, tracing the lines of it, the beautiful wound…

"Lia, Lia," he whispered, "you are going to make my life very interesting this week."

She sat back and put some space between them.

"Will I have to share you with other patrons?"

He shook his head. "For you I'm clearing my whole calendar."

She smiled, though she tried not to let him see it.

"You're so beautiful," she said.

"That's kind of you to say."

"Credit where credit's due," she said, and cleared her throat.

He slid his hand under her chin, lifted it.

"I'm not going to force you to do anything you don't want to do this week," he said. "I don't force. I seduce. But I will seduce you, and by the end of the week you will have done things with me you never dreamed you wanted to do. You understand?"

She slowly nodded.

"Let's get into bed," he said. "I want you on my cock."

She took another heaving breath. She might have squeaked.

"You're a grown woman, Lia. You're allowed to have sex and enjoy it."

"It was so easy to be with you before."

"Because I was someone else?"

"Because *I* was someone else," she said. "I don't know if I can..."

"You can. You will. But we can go slowly. Bring the cup. I'll fetch the wine."

Lia relaxed slightly when August stepped away from her. She busied herself opening her bag and taking out the kylix, which she'd wrapped up carefully in clean linen. She carried it over to the bed.

August came up behind and pressed himself against her back. He took the cup from her hand and set it on the black square nightstand, next to an open bottle of red wine. He wrapped his arms around her stomach and kissed the side of her neck.

The warmth of his body seeped through the fabric of her dress and into her skin. She stood still, too nervous to move, as he nibbled the pulse point in her neck and ran his hands slowly up and down her back. She liked it but didn't know how to respond. And she wanted to respond. She wanted him to know she wanted him.

"Relax," he said into her ear, as if he'd read her thoughts. "Let me do my job. And let me show you why I love my work."

She smiled, nodded, still nervous but relieved she wouldn't be expected to perform.

"But first, let us bid adieu to your clothes."

"No," she said, turning to face him. "No. No, no, no."

He narrowed his eyes at her. "You do know how sex works, yes?"

She held up her hand and pushed the air, demanding some room between them. He obliged and took one step back.

Lia unzipped her dress, pulled it off and laid it over the back of a chair. Under it, she wore a simple ivory slip, one that had belonged to her grandmother in the `60s.

"Better." He stepped forward and ran his hands over her back again and Lia shivered pleasantly as his skin warmed her through the silk. "This is very pretty. It will look even prettier on my floor..."

"Give me time," she said.

"All the time you need," he said, and kissed her neck again. "But we're getting rid of the knickers right this second."

She made a sound halfway between a whimper and a squeak.

They had a deal, she reminded herself.

"All right."

August pulled her knickers down her legs and with a dainty lift of her feet she was out of them.

"Not so bad, was it?" he asked after tossing her underwear all the way across the room.

"I survived."

"Now would you be so kind as to bend over the bed?"

"Why?"

"It will make lubricating your vagina easier."

Another small sound came out of Lia's throat, like air escaping a balloon.

"Or you could lie on your back," he suggested.

He was trying to be helpful.

"I'll just…um…do the first one," she said.

With as much grace and dignity as she could muster under the circumstances—weird bed, weird bedroom, weird yet incredibly attractive naked male prostitute standing behind her with an erection—Lia bent over the bed.

"I'm not going to spank your arse," he said as he lifted the back of her slip.

"Thank you."

"Unless you want me to."

"Let's table that for now."

He didn't say anything. That troubled her. Deeply.

"You're looking at my vagina, aren't you?" she asked.

"Yes."

She sighed.

"It's very pretty." He touched the seam of her vulva and lightly stroked it with his fingertip. It parted at his touch and Lia's fingers curled into the bedspread. "Beautiful cunt."

Lia grimaced. "Do you really have to call it that?"

"Yes. You should, too. It's sexy."

"It's rude."

"Sexy."

"Crude."

"Prissiest madam ever, I swear to the gods."

Lia heard him opening a drawer and felt the first touch of warm liquid on her body.

"I thought it would be cold," she said.

"I have a lube-warmer."

"Of course you do."

She tensed as he spread her labia open wider. He made

a sound like "Hmm…"—the sound of an art critic judging a painting.

"What?" she demanded.

"Your cunt looks like a rose," he said.

"Does not."

"Pink-red petals, dark little center, bit dewy."

Lia buried her burning face against the cool suede of his bedspread.

August touched a tender spot inside her.

Lia gasped as her vagina clenched around his fingers.

August laughed. Wonderful laugh.

"I'm falling in love with you already," he said.

"Well. Stop," she said. "Please and thank you."

"Prude."

"Are you finished now?"

"I am," he said. "And you really didn't need the lube. You were soaking wet before I got there."

He pulled his fingers out of her—bad—and Lia stood up—good.

She turned to face August, who was using a little white towel to wipe his fingers clean.

"Now what?" she asked. She was feeling quite…slippery.

"I need to know what sexual fantasy you'd like to experience tonight."

"Don't rush me," she said. "This is my session, isn't it?"

He put his hands together in a prayer position. "I am all yours."

"Thank you. I thought so."

"What would you like to do, Lia?" he asked, the picture of submission.

Damn him…he'd called her bluff.

"Well...I'm open to suggestions," she said. August managed not to laugh at her too loudly.

"Probably a good idea to get started," he said. "Before you lose your nerve."

Lia nodded. "Agreed."

He slipped into bed and propped himself against the tufted leather headboard. How was he so comfortable being naked while she was shaking in her slip?

"Could you pass the condoms, please?" he asked.

He'd put an entire box of them on the nightstand. Felt rude, like bragging. Surely they wouldn't need more than one. She passed him one.

One.

"Lia? You're there." He pointed at the floor. "I require your presence here." He patted his stomach. Lia slowly crawled onto the bed, wishing the entire time August had a much bigger bed.

"Why is your bed so small?" she asked.

"More intimate. You can hide from someone in a king-size. Not in this bed. No hiding places at all..."

He reached for her and, with his hands on her waist, pulled her on top of him. She sat on his stomach and found herself *very* aware of her wet bare vulva pressing against his warm flesh. She was trying to ignore his cock, though it certainly wasn't ignoring her.

Lia was of two minds. One mind wanted to get her things and rush straight home and pretend she never had this terrible idea. The other mind wanted to press her entire body to August's entire body and stay there a few millennia. August took her face in his hands, stroked her cheeks, her neck. Then he smiled at her.

Might as well stay, she decided.

"It won't hurt," he said.

"I'm not a virgin."

"That's not what I meant, and you know it." He brushed her hair over her shoulder and leaned in to kiss her. His lips met hers and Lia shivered. She clung awkwardly to his shoulders as she returned the kiss, tentatively at first but with growing confidence. August ran his fingertips up her arms and over her shoulders, across her back and down to her waist. The man kissed like he invented kissing, patented it and made a fortune off the patent. He nipped her bottom lip, dipped his tongue into her mouth and retreated, pushed and retreated, teasing her until there was nothing for her to do but put her own tongue in his mouth. That would show him.

When her tongue met his, August moaned softly. He pulled her closer and Lia could almost swear he wanted her as much as she wanted him. Of course he didn't. This was the job, and she knew how it worked. And that was fine. She wasn't here to fall in love. She knew better than that, and even if she didn't, she knew she couldn't.

But…she could enjoy herself while it lasted, right?

"You're a good kisser," August whispered.

"I was thinking the same about you."

He smiled again, and looked in her eyes again, making her blush again.

"What?" she asked.

"You're insanely beautiful."

"Shut up. I have a gap in my two front teeth."

"Like Isabella Rossellini."

"Like David Letterman," she retorted.

"It's a sign of a strong libido. Ask the Wife of Bath. And very, very sexy."

He kissed her again, before she could tell him all the ways he was wrong about that. And as he kissed her, he slowly and with the utmost care moved her so that she was on top of his cock.

"Take your time," he said.

Lia pushed a lock of hair out of her face and tucked it behind her ear.

"So…" she began. "Help?"

He really had the most wonderful smile when he was trying not to laugh at her. Lia could get used to that smile—when she got over the urge to wipe it off his face.

"Allow me," he said. He took her by the waist and gently pulled her down until she was sitting on his erection.

He reached under her slip and took himself in hand. With one hand on her and the other on his cock, and with a judicious lift of his hips, the tip found the entrance of her body and pressed against the tender hole. With her hands on his shoulders, she moved up and then forward as August pressed up and into her.

Accidentally—she was trying to look anywhere but at August—she met his eyes while steadying herself against the headboard. And once he had her attention, he didn't let her look away.

He wasn't smiling now, but the expression on his face was somehow better than a smile. His eyes were soft as he gazed at her face, and his hands gentle as he lifted her hips and guided her onto him. Lia felt pressure as she lowered herself onto his cock. Pressure and penetration as he entered her slowly, inch by inch, until she'd taken as much of him as she could. She rocked back and forth simply to make herself more comfortable.

August must have liked it because his eyelids fluttered, and his back arched against the pillows. Beautiful man.

"There," he said, panting slightly. He put his hand on the side of her face and stroked her cheek with this thumb. "That's not so bad, is it?"

Lia swallowed. "It's all right. Not bad."

The lacy hem of her slip lay over her thighs as she knelt on him. August slid his hands under it again.

"Do you want to make love?" he asked. "Or talk about your fantasies?"

"You're a man. Don't you need to come?"

"I'm not a normal man. I can stay hard for a very long time. Especially if a beautiful young woman is sitting on my cock and blushing pink as a rose. If I start to get soft, I'll just peek."

"Peek?"

He lifted her hem, and she slapped it back down again.

"Do not peek."

"Lia, I'm literally penetrating you right this moment. We are having sexual intercourse. We are fornicating."

"Fine," she said. "You can peek." He really did feel very good inside her. The cock in her throbbed and her flesh surrounding it throbbed in time. She placed her hands flat on his chest and rocked her hips into his. She was rewarded with a deep spasm inside her stomach, a spasm that traveled up her spine and down into her thighs. She braced herself, her hands flat on August's broad chest, and did it again.

"Take your slip off," he said, his voice hoarse. He was already inside her. There was no reason for her to feel modest, but her fingers were shaking as she tried for the zipper in back. He grew impatient with her fumbling fingers and pulled it down for her. When he'd bared her breasts, he looked at them so long and so longingly Lia blushed.

"You're staring," she said.

"Phryne of Athens," he said. "The courtesan. When she was charged with impiety and taken before the courts, she bared her breasts to the judges. At the sight of them, they acquitted her. At the sight of your breasts, they would have crowned you empress."

He squeezed them, molded them into his palms, fondled the nipples until they were so hard she hurt. He wrapped his arms around her waist. Her head fell back and she arched for him, gasping as he licked her left nipple, placed his lips to it and sucked it into his mouth. The slow draw, the tug, the moist heat on her breast, was bliss.

For the first time, Lia felt the line, the red cord of nerves that ran from her breasts to her sex. As he sucked the nipple, drew it deep into his mouth, her vagina grew wetter, riper, swollen.

She pressed her hips against him and felt the pleasure run down her back and into her hips. August pulled her against him again and pushed his hand between her thighs. Lia's vagina ached around the thick organ inside her, and she moaned against his shoulder.

Never had she felt this good before, not in her own body. He took her breasts in his hands again—his large, strong male hands—and held them firmly. She covered his hands with hers, wanting to feel him touching her. Lowering her head, she pressed a quick kiss onto his knuckles. That one kiss, no matter how devout, wasn't nearly enough for August. He grinned that wild dangerous grin of his again. He kissed her again with that wild dangerous kiss of his.

August wrapped an arm around her and scored her back with his rough fingertips. She'd never felt something so sensuous. Every time she moved, even the slightest bit, her clitoris brushed the shaft of his cock.

"August," she said.

"Yes?"

"What?" she asked.

"You said my name."

"I did?"

He slowly nodded. She forced her eye to focus.

"Stop gloating." She'd been clinging to the headboard, but August took her hands by the wrists and brought them down to his stomach.

"I can't help it," he said. "You're beautiful and I'm arrogant. This is so much fun I can't believe I get paid for it."

"Are you really enjoying this?"

In lieu of answering, he rolled her onto her back on the bed.

"August—"

He took her legs and wrapped them around his lower back. Then he pried her hands off his upper arms and pressed them into the bed. To make matters worse, he put his hands over her hands, and locked their fingers together.

"You're trying to make me feel something for you," Lia said. "I know all the tricks."

"I feel something for you already," August said. "And this isn't a trick."

Slowly, and very deliberately, he began to thrust into her.

Slowly, and very deliberately, he let his full weight rest on her until she could think of nothing and no one but him.

"Remember what I said about the Fates?" he asked. A kiss on her lips. A kiss on her cheek. A kiss on her neck. "About the threads of our destinies being tangled together?"

"You really believe that?" Her voice was breathless. His thrusts were so incredibly deep and slow she couldn't help but move with him.

"We're tangled together right now. Can't you feel it?"

She nodded, too turned on to speak. He released her right hand and brushed her hair off her cheek and then cradled the back of her head. August pushed his knees in until they were at her hips. He'd tangled them together in a tight, tense knot of arms and legs and a hundred deep kisses.

"How's this for a Gordian knot?" he said into her ear as he thrust into her again. Lia arched under him.

He kissed her mouth, deeper even than before. Their tongues touched and mingled as August moved in her with long slow strokes of his cock.

"We can stop if you want to," he said. "Do you?"

She shook her head. "No."

August smiled down at her, caressed her cheek with the back of his knuckles.

"I don't know what he did to you," he said, "but I'm going to enjoy undoing it."

"You can't change the past."

"No, but I can give you a very good present." He thrust into her again.

She laughed, a real laugh, deep and throaty and sensual. She sounded like a woman who was enjoying herself. He laughed with her, dropping dozens of tender kisses on her neck and along her collarbone. All right...so maybe he did want her. She relaxed underneath him and spread her thighs a little wider.

"Shall we play?" he asked. "I think the wine's breathed enough."

"What do I do?"

"Tell me your sexual fantasy you want to explore tonight."

Lia tensed again. Two steps forward, one step back.

"You first," she said.

"I'm a wicked king," he said immediately.

"Oh my God." How many of these insane sexual fantasies did he have?

"And a very powerful king at that," he continued. "And there's another lesser king who has to send tribute to me. But this poor king has no gold or silver or diamonds to send me. All he has that I might desire is..."

"His daughter?"

"His *only* daughter," August said. "She's sent to me to be my concubine."

"It's never a secretary, is it? Or a juggler? The tribute always has to be a concubine."

"And when she arrives at my palace, because I am so very wicked, I make her strip naked and show herself to me in front of the entire court."

"You're an absolute bastard. Worst king since Nero."

"Nero was an emperor, not a king," he said. "But don't

worry, she gets her revenge. When I make love to her the first night…she tries to stab me with a dagger she's hidden under the pillow."

"Good girl. I like her spirit."

"But I'm not deterred."

"Quitters never win," she said.

"I decide that I can't simply overwhelm her with power and might. I must make her love me. So begins my attempt to win her heart and obedience through a strict regimen of hand-feeding, spankings followed by forced orgasms, and tender poetry."

"Poetry?"

"Yes, I tie her to the royal bed and recite poems to her until her heart—and thighs—melt."

"This is an actual sexual fantasy you get off to?" Lia asked.

"Often." August nodded. "Though there are variations. Sometimes it's the king's son instead of his daughter. And instead of poetry, it's near-constant oral sex."

"I'm speechless."

"Your turn," he said, his voice tender and coaxing. "I'm dying to hear what you dream about in that deep dark little corner of your mind, the one with all the locks on the door and Cerberus guarding it with all three of his vicious heads…"

He massaged her breasts as he spoke, and she did find herself strangely melting into his hands.

"Close your eyes, Lia," he said as he then pushed his hands gently into her hair and tugged her head back to bare her throat to another hundred soft kisses.

She closed her eyes and sighed at the bliss of the moment—his beautiful cock embedded in her body, his fingers wound into her hair, his warm lips licking and sucking her neck and his hot breath on her skin… And his words, his perfect words.

"Tell me your secrets, Lia…tell me everything you want. I won't laugh. I won't judge. Whatever you desire, I can give it to you, but you have to tell me what it is…"

"You won't laugh?"

"I really won't laugh."

"Well, to be honest…I wouldn't mind playing in your fantasy."

"You'd make a wonderful wicked king."

She opened her eyes and looked at him. "The bloody concubine, August."

He pulled back, his eyes wide. "You disgust me."

Lia pushed him off her. That act of rebellion was quickly quashed. August grabbed her around the waist, wrenched her slip off her and threw it across the room. Then he dragged her on top of him, and it took no convincing at all to get her to straddle him.

"So she wants to be a concubine," August said. He took her by the hips and eased her down onto him again.

"No, I don't want to be a bloody concubine," she said. "It's a fancy word for being a victim of kidnapping and rape."

"But you fantasize about being kidnapped and raped."

"In a nice way." She let her head fall back and smiled dreamily up at the ceiling. "A sexy way. A not-at-all-real-in-any-way way. That's what I meant."

He ran his hands up her arms and drew her down to his chest.

"Who do you imagine being your keeper? Your captor?"

"Achilles," she said.

"Ah, does that make you Briseis?" he asked.

"I think I'd make a very good captive queen."

Achilles and his best friend and shield-bearer Patroclus were her two favorite characters in *The Iliad*. She loved how much they loved each other, protected each other. And from her first reading, she'd secretly envied Briseis, the enemy queen who Achilles took as his personal concubine.

"Let's find out."

Still underneath her, August reached for the kylix and wine bottle on the bedside table. He splashed in a little wine and offered the cup to her. Lia's heart beat madly as she took it from him and cradled it in her hands.

"Ready?" he asked. She took a shuddering breath.

"Ready as I'll ever be."

Her toes were already curling in anticipation and excitement. But fear, too. Real fear. What on earth was about to happen to her?

Lia lifted the kylix to her lips and drank deeply. Her hands shook so badly August took the cup back from her. He drank from it and set it on the table again. Then he rolled them over so that he lay on top of her again.

"Nervous?" he asked.

"Very."

"You'll be safe," he said. "I won't let anything happen to you except the preauthorized capture and very pleasant rape."

"Good, thank you."

"Until then…" He kissed her deeply on the mouth, and his tongue tasted of wine. She wrapped her arms around his back and held on to him tightly. Before she knew what she was doing, Lia opened her thighs for him again.

August entered her with a thrust.

"My lovely concubine," he said.

"You're more my concubine than I'm yours. I bought you."

"Rented," he said. "Do you really want to play my concubine, or did you just want to see me in a leather kilt?"

"It's called a pteruges," Lia said.

August laughed softly into her ear. "I know what it's called, and you didn't answer my question."

Lia started to answer it, but before she could speak another word, the world went dark.

———

THE STORY CONTINUES in The Rose, *available now in trade paperback, ebook, and audio from Harlequin's Mira Books and Harper Audio.*

A PEARL NECKLACE

EXCERPT FROM "THE PEARL"

When Lord Arthur Godwick learns his younger brother is up to his bollocks in debt to Regan Ferry, owner of The Pearl Hotel, he agrees to work off the tab...in her bed. Soon the handsome but troubled Arthur discovers he's a pawn in an erotic game of revenge—and nothing, including his lover, is what it seems.

THE
PEARL

Arthur went out to the garden terrace to find Regan. He followed a lantern-lit path to the bird perch where Gloom was happily dipping his enormous black beak into a bowl of raw and bloody meat.

"I begin to understand," Arthur said, "the origins of the term *'raven*ously.'"

"Hungry little buggars, aren't they? Ravens originally came to London from the country, drawn to the carcasses of animals that used to float along the Thames from the slaughterhouses."

"But a pet raven," Arthur said. "How does that happen?"

Regan looked over her shoulder, smiled at him as she held out her arm and let the bird climb onto her wrist.

"Gloom landed on the terrace with a bent wing, and I brought in a wildlife rehabilitator to help him. Ravens have wonderful memories for humans who help them." She stroked Gloom lightly across the back of his head.

"Does he bite?"

"Of course they bite. Better to get bitten by a hawk than a raven. See?"

She held out her right hand to show a pale white scar near her wrist. "He nipped me good and hard when I had to catch him that first day he landed with the broken wing."

"That must have hurt," he said and touched the scar, gently caressing it. "But you kept him anyway."

"He was scared. Animals bite when they're scared."

"Is that why you bite, because you're scared?"

She stared at him, darkly, coldly. "I know you're trying to make me like you," she said. "It won't happen."

"I think it's happening."

"It will *never* happen."

He lowered his voice to a haunted house whisper. "It's already begun…"

That got her to laugh, a little. A very little, but still he counted it as a win.

"Come on, Brat. Time to work off more of your brother's debt." She left her bird to his bloody feast and went back into the suite.

He followed her up the curving staircase to the red and gold bedroom. She opened the door and let him inside, and the first thing he saw was his great-grandfather's portrait hanging across from the bed, uncovered. He groaned.

"Don't ask me to cover him up again," Regan said and went to the fireplace and turned on the gas. "You'll simply have to get used to having an audience."

"He's my great-grandfather. Having him here is the exact opposite of taking Viagra."

"He's a man you've never even met, who has been dead for over eighty years."

"Fine. Leave it," Arthur said. "Let's put on a show."

"He'd appreciate that. Loved to watch other people fucking almost as much as he loved being watched."

"This is not helping me to get aroused here," Arthur reminded her.

"You're already half-hard in your jeans and don't deny it."

"Not a full half. Maybe a third."

She pointed at the parcel he was carrying. "Is that the artwork you brought to play in honor of dear old great-granddad?"

"I did. Sort of. It's only a signed lithograph. We have a

Georgia O'Keeffe, but skulls aren't nearly as erotic as her flowers."

He unwrapped the cover from the print and gave it to Regan who set it atop the fireplace mantel.

The painting was called *Black Iris III*—an iris, painted in extreme closeup, its petals a lurid purple, so dark they almost look black. And the flower was open, blooming, wide and trembling.

"A boy never forgets his first O'Keeffe," he said.

"Yes, because it looks like an enormous engorged cunt."

"It's a very nice enormous engorged cunt."

She looked at him, eyebrow slightly raised. "I think that's the first time I've heard you say the word 'cunt' in my presence."

"Might be the first time I've ever said it out loud. When you're the son of Spencer Godwick, you rebel by *not* being rude."

"I like it. You should say it more. Use it in a sentence."

"Now?"

She nodded.

"Ah…I would like to do very nice things to your cunt."

"Now a question."

"May I please do very nice things to your cunt?"

Regan came to him, stood in front of him.

"Yes," she said. "You may do very nice things to my cunt."

"I serve at your pleasure," he said, not entirely without sarcasm.

"Yes, yes you do." She put her hands on his shoulders and leaned back, smiling at the portrait of Lord Malcolm. "Did you hear that, Malcolm? I've turned your great-grandson into a whore. Who are you prouder of? Him or me?"

"You are insane," Arthur said. He really wished she would stop talking to the painting. It wouldn't be good if it started talking back.

She smiled at him, then brought her hand between them, cupping his crotch.

"And you're hard," she said. "Guess having great-granddad here isn't as much as a mood-killer as you thought, is it?"

She kissed him and no amount of wounded male pride could keep from kissing her back. She wasn't cruel to him so much as she was just…cold, and it seemed at the moment he'd started to shiver, she would turn hot, hot and burning. And the colder she was to him, the more he wanted her. And the more he wanted her, the colder she was to him. Even this, hanging his great-grandfather's portrait was cruel, made him feel vulnerable, exposed, and what she exposed was how much he loved being exposed.

He returned the kiss, pushing his tongue into her mouth, tasting her.

"You like this so much," she said against his lips, laughing between kisses. "You like being treated like this and I love it. I love it and you hate it."

"I hate that I love it," he said soft as a penitent giving his confession. He wrapped his fingers around her long pearl necklace and lightly, lightly, oh-so lightly tugged on it to make sure he had her attention. "But I like that you like it."

If only she liked him a little. Maybe? A little? She smiled, a real one, not mocking and it was gone as fast as it had come.

"Get on your knees," she said.

She said it so he did it. He released his grip on her pearls and went down onto his knees in front of her. As soon as he was there, he realized this is where he'd wanted to be all along.

"You whore," she said, and cupped him under the chin. "Did I make you like this? Or were you like this before me?"

"I was like this before you, but I don't want to be like this after you."

"Why not? You're enjoying it as much as I am."

"I just...don't." If he could have waved a wand to make it go away, he would have waved it like a drowning man signaling for help. Once Regan was done with him, who would treat him like this? Who could he trust to tell that he needed it? Where would he begin to find someone who made him feel what Regan did?

"Who told you this was wrong?" she asked him.

"What?"

"Someone must have gotten it in your head that this, what we're doing, is wrong, bad, the sort of thing real men don't do? Who was it?"

"Nobody. You know the Godwicks. We're one big happy whoring family."

Regan stared him down, but he refused to be goaded into answering.

"Do you want to keep glaring at me," he asked, "or do you want me to make you come?"

"Well, when you put it that way," she said and finally smiled. Then she grabbed him hard by the chin, hard enough he knew she'd leave red marks from the rough grip of her fingers. "But make it good."

He met her eyes. "I'll make it good."

Gently, he pressed his mouth to her stomach and felt the soft muscles fluttering. His hands found her ankles, fragile and birdlike. He stroked up her bare legs, up her calves, up her thighs, under her little black dress to her little black lace pants underneath. He held her soft small arse in his hands as he kissed the mouth at the apex of her thighs through her dress as he started to pull her knickers down. When they were at her ankles, she lightly kicked them aside. Then she stepped back and sat on the edge of the bed.

She crooked her finger and he crawled across the floor, only two feet but it felt like two miles on a public street, just from the humiliation of it. The delicious humiliation.

It was worth it for the reward at the finish line, to push her thighs apart and press between them. He lifted up the skirt of her dress and tucked it under her to keep it out of his way. There she was, the soft light brown hair on her mound and the seam he'd touched and fucked but hadn't tasted yet. He buried his face against her warm thighs, inhaled the light musky scent of her arousal. He kissed the curls of her sex as he pushed her legs apart. His fingers found the slit of her vulva and he stroked it slowly, carefully. Then he opened the folds, parting them like petals. And they *were* like petals, silky and warm as if in sunlight.

He spread the folds of her labia wider. His mouth watered. Lowering his head, he pressed his tongue to her vulva, tasting his first drop of her. One drop wasn't enough, so he licked her, drawing his tongue up and receiving as his reward Regan's arm around the back of his head, her hand in his hair.

"More," she said, a quiet and gentle order. She wanted more, and she would get more.

Arthur cupped her bottom again and pulled her to the edge of the bed. She rolled back as he lifted her legs, setting her feet on the bed so that her thighs fell wide, wide open.

The light from the bedside lamp showed her cunt in all its glory as he pulled the labia apart again, spreading them open. Regan's breathing quickened. She liked this, being opened, being seen. Had her old husband even been able to fuck her, or did he just keep her on his arm to make the world think he could satisfy a woman like Regan?

Her clitoris was hidden under a little shield of skin. He lightly rubbed around it, the tips of his two fingers on either side, rubbing it in circles. She inhaled a long breath and held it. The tight knot of flesh swelled under his touch and in the lamplight he could see the clitoris itself starting to come out from hiding. As carefully as he could he pulled that hood of flesh back, exposing the tiny knot. He brought the very, very tip of his tongue to it. Regan gasped at the gentle contact. He licked it again, a little harder and then again, again, again. Her clitoris swelled more, blooming before his eyes.

He pushed a finger into her vagina. Inside she was slick and scalding hot. He needed more of that heat on him. He pushed in a second finger, then a third. Was there anything more beautiful than seeing her open cunt wrapped around his hand? If she'd been more open he might have tried working his entire fist inside of her. But she was too taut, too tight. He pushed against the clenching muscles inside her and they pushed back.

"Are you seeing this, Lord Malcolm?" Regan said. She

spoke to the painting, but her gaze was locked on Arthur's eyes. "You see how your family has fallen? You used to buy women for your pleasure like a kid in a candy shop and now here's your heir worshipping at the cunt of the great-granddaughter of a whore."

Her arrogant tone was like petrol tossed on a fire and he was the fire.

Arthur's cock throbbed inside his pants. As he licked her cunt, he unzipped his jeans, freed his erection from the confines of his clothes. He wanted to climb on her, mount and enter her, but he didn't, of course, though the urge to fill her with come was painfully strong. To release into her ropes of thick white come and then to pull out and to see his own semen dripping out of her…

Arthur kissed a path up her body, up her belly, coming up high on his knees and kissing her neck.

He took the long string of pearls around her neck and started to take them off of her.

"What are you doing?" she asked.

"You told me to make it good."

She gave him a look but didn't argue and surrendered her pearls to him. Her face was flushed and her pupils so wide and dilated, she had black irises, just as she'd wanted.

He kissed her once on the mouth, letting her taste herself before going down on his knees again.

The pearls were heavy in his hand. True saltwater pearls, a fortune in pearls. He poured them into his hand, and they filled his entire fist.

He pushed her thighs open again, kissed and licked her clitoris until she was moaning. But it wasn't enough to make her moan. He wanted her to scream.

Arthur began to push the pearls into her cunt.

At first it was clear she didn't understand what he was doing. Then at once, she understood and rose up on her elbows. She didn't say anything, didn't stop him, just watched. He looked at her once and saw her face, her eyes, looking at her own open cunt, her thighs wide, heels braced on the edge of the bed.

Pearl by pearl, inch by inch, he pushed the strand into her, filling her hole with enough pearls to pay a year's rent on a two-bedroom flat in Mayfair. And she let him.

She lay back as more pearls filled her, too many to count. She lay back and let him push the entire long strand into her. It took time. God knows how long but she lay there and panted while he did it, panted and pulled at the bedcovers. He saw her fingers nearly tearing the silk as she twisted her hands into the fabric.

"Too much?" he asked.

"Too much. It's perfect."

And that was Regan. Enough was not enough. Too much was perfect. He pushed in the last of the pearls. They split her cunt open so that he could see the small shining white beads straining her hole as her inner muscles stretched to accommodate them. He put his hand flat over her opening to keep them in.

Then he licked her clitoris again. It was so swollen he didn't even have to hold the hood back to get to the naked organ. Regan's hips rose in tight and tiny undulations. She was coming undone, utterly undone. Her breathing grew louder, and her head moved on the bed. She made sounds, beautiful pained sounds but didn't ask him to stop, only spread her legs wider.

He licked her hard. She was long gone now. He

thought about stopping, to punish her, but it would have punished him more to stop licking her, kneading her pulsing little clit with his tongue as she pushed her hips up and into his mouth.

She came with a sudden jerk of her body and a gasp. Her head rose off the bed, head and shoulders, before she fell back panting, still softly moaning. Her thighs fell open. She went limp and Arthur let the pearls begin to fall out of her body, one loop dangling out a few inches. He caught the loop in his finger—the pearls were damp—and gently he pulled on them, emptying her out. Her vagina gave little gasps, little twitches. He gathered the long string of her pearls into his hands as he pulled them out of her and then she was empty. He stood and gazed down on her, her dressed ruched up to her waist, her eyes closed, her body listless and spent.

Arthur straddled her, pushed his cock into her dripping opening and when she didn't stop him, he entered her with a stroke. Her cunt was open now, supple and soft against his cock. It was ecstasy to feel her body taking every inch of him without any resistance. He was bathed in heat and wetness. She lay motionless under him, insensate, eyes half-closed, letting him have her. He pounded fast, rutting on her, ashamed of his lack of self-control but not ashamed enough to stop. His thrusts were pistons firing fast and hard and it was only seconds until he started to come. He pulled out. Gripping his cock in his hand, he came on Regan's neck. Spurts of semen landed white and wet on her glistening olive skin, on her chest, in the hollow of her throat, and each spurt was harder and stronger than the last.

When he'd finished emptying himself out onto her, he

looked at her, at what he'd done and decided he'd seen no work of art in the world more beautiful than this woman wearing his come.

"I'll clean you off," he said. "Lay there."

"No," she said. "Leave it."

He slid to the floor, to his knees again and rested his head on her lower stomach. Regan slowly moved her legs, spreading them again. She sat up, still wearing his come and opened her vulva wide open for him.

Her cunt was a livid red, almost purple, tender from how hard he'd used her and supple enough to spread out wide as an iris in bloom.

"Well done, Brat," she said and touched his burning face. He kissed her thigh. She dug her hands into his hair and stroked it tenderly. Then she picked up the pearls and examined them, shaking her head.

"I'll clean your pearls," he said, smiling sheepishly. "I promise."

She put them on over her head and let them settle around her neck.

"No. I'll wear them just like this."

THE STORY CONTINUES in The Pearl, *available now in trade paperback, ebook, library hardcover binding, and audiobook from 8th Circle Press and Tantor Audio.*

THE BEGUILING OF MERLIN
THE COMPLETE SHORT STORY

A standalone erotic short story from Tiffany Reisz that ties into the first Godwicks novel, The Red. *First published in* Best Bondage Erotica of the Year, Vol. 1, *edited by Rachel Kramer Bussel, and later issued in print as a standalone paperback with* The Pearl *pre-order bundle. "The Beguiling of Merlin" is presented here in its entirety.*

The Beguiling of Merlin

Mona entered her private office at the Red, her little art gallery on Savoy Street. She'd come in search of a missing invoice, but the invoice was forgotten completely when she spied a book of Pre-Raphaelite art plates on her desk, a red ribbon marking a page.

Mona's heart danced and her blood heated as she saw that red satin tongue sticking out of those cream-colored pages. This was her lover Malcolm's game. When he was in the mood to fuck her, he left a painting on her desk as a hint, sometimes a challenge. Whatever was in the painting, that was how he'd have her that night. One night it had been *The Slave Market* by French artist Jean-Léon Gérôme, and her body had been auctioned off to the highest bidder—Malcolm, of course. Another night they'd sported in a sacred grove as she'd played nymph to his satyr in honor of the famous painting *Nymphs and Satyr* by the old master William-Adolphe Bouguereau.

What was it to be tonight?

Mona let the anticipation build as she sat primly in her desk chair and pinned a wayward strand of candy-apple-red hair into the knot at the nape of her neck. She forced herself to flip through all the pages of the art book and not turn right to the marked page. Mona had always adored the Pre-Raphaelites, those painters who were obsessed, it seemed, with beauty and beauty alone. The paintings had no meaning, no message, and no morality, not unlike Malcolm. The artists simply loved painting beautiful things—lakes, oceans, magical houses, lovely long-limbed boys, and beautiful women, usually their mistresses.

Finally Mona turned to the marked page.

Ah. This was a new game—*The Beguiling of Merlin* by

Edward Burne-Jones, one of the last of the Pre-Raphaelite painters. Mona knew this painting and loved it. It showed a woman of rare power, Viviane, the famous Lady of the Lake from Arthurian legends. In the painting, the Lady of the Lake had tricked the wizard Merlin in some way so she could bind him in the branches of a spiky hawthorn bush and steal his book of magic.

How fitting. Malcolm was very much a Merlin who worked strange erotic magic on Mona every time they had their trysts in the back room of the Red. Malcolm hadn't just marked the painting in the book. He'd left a note for her as well. She unfolded a crisp white note card and read, *If you can steal my book of magic as Viviane stole Merlin's, you'll know how I do all my tricks.*

The note was signed, *All my lust, Malcolm.*

How could Mona resist that challenge? She'd wondered for months now how Malcolm worked his magic, how he transformed the back room of her art gallery into the paintings they played in whenever he was in the mood to use her body. At first she simply thought he was wealthy enough to put on lifelike plays for their pleasure alone. But as the months passed and the fantasies they explored grew more elaborate and terrifyingly real, she had to admit there was only one explanation for how it was done—magic.

Mona examined the painting in the book again. In it, the Lady of the Lake wore a gauzy gown of blue-gray. Mona had a nightgown that would do nicely. She returned to her apartment and found it in her closet. At midnight, she returned to the Red. In her office, she quickly changed into the gauzy gown, eager to see her mysterious magical lover again.

She opened the door to the gallery's back room, which was nothing more than a storage room—usually. But when Malcolm wanted to work his magic, he could turn the back room into anything—an auction house, a sacred grove, a labyrinth, a Roman prison.

Mona stepped across the threshold and onto soft grass. She shut the door behind her and found herself in an enchanted spring forest.

How? How did Malcolm do it? She had to know. If she beguiled her "Merlin" well enough, perhaps she would learn his secrets before the night was over.

But first…she had to find him.

Mona dug her naked toes into the spongy ground and glanced around at the mossy trees that towered fifty feet or more above her. The air smelled clean and pure, dew wet and dreamy, like the first morning breeze off an ancient unspoiled lake.

She heard the lapping and laughing of water nearby. Mona ran toward it, remembering that in this fantasy she was the Lady of the Lake. And if she was the Lady of the Lake, she needed her lake, didn't she?

Mona rushed through the woods until she came to the rocky lakeshore. The lake stretched far and wide before her, glinting in the dawn light. And across the lake on the opposite shore, she spied a man in a dark-blue cloak disappearing between two trees.

As she was the Lady of the Lake, it was nothing to walk across the water. Once on the other side, she slipped into the woods and found a hawthorn bush with vicious thorns aplenty. Across from the bush stood an ancient gnarled yew tree, with branches so low they scraped the ground. She took the blue scarf from her hair and used it to loosely tie her wrists to a branch above her head.

"Help?" she cried out. "Help me, please!"

She tried not to laugh as she cried out for help. This was the hardest part, keeping a straight face as they played their games.

Hardly a minute passed before Malcolm stepped into the clearing. He stared at her, clearly amused by her pitiful attempt to play damsel in distress. She burned with desire at the sight of him—the black hair in the roguish wave, with a touch of silver at the temples, the strong nose and jaw, the dark glinting mischievous eyes, the hands that knew all the secrets of her body...she had to have him. Now.

"You require help, my lady?" he asked.

"A wicked knight in stolen armor captured me," she said, "as I was out picking berries. Please, untie me before he returns and takes me away with him."

The scarf was so loose around her wrists, she could have slipped her hands from the loops. She thought if she could take Malcolm—Merlin—unawares, she could push him backward into the hawthorn bush where he would be trapped by the thorns. If only he would take the bait...

She was the bait.

Under his cloak, Malcolm wore rough canvas trousers and a linen tunic. He did a very good job of looking like an ordinary Jack-of-the-Green and not the wicked magician she knew he truly was. He took off his cloak and hung it over a branch. She spied his leather-bound book of magic tucked inside a pocket in the cloak lining.

"A wicked knight in stolen armor," he repeated, his

tone mocking. "And you...out picking berries. I see no footprints of a knight. I see no berries."

He stepped closer to her, so close they would have been eye to eye were he not a head taller than Mona. He raised his hand to her neck and caught a curling red lock of her hair around his finger. He lifted the lock to his nose.

"I'm not so sure I should release you," Malcolm said. "No berries. No footprints. You could very well be a witch."

"I am no witch," she said. "Only a maiden, far from home."

"A maiden?" he repeated. "A maiden in the woods should smell of earth and soap. You smell of water lilies. I don't think you're a maiden at all. A maiden would blush."

"You've given me no reason to blush."

"Then I shall."

He grinned a devilish, wicked grin as he stroked her cheek with the back of his hand. She warmed at his touch but didn't blush. The things he'd done to her during their nights together had taken away all her shame. She couldn't blush if she tried. But for the sake of the game, she did try.

"No blushes," he said as he pressed his body against hers, pushing her back into the rough trunk of the yew tree. The scarf on her wrist tightened its grip. She could still escape, however, if she wanted to.

If...

"I'd hardly blush from the merest touch of a man's hand on my face. I'm a maiden," she said, "not a child."

"Ah, but there's other ways to find out if a lady is a maiden as she claims." His warm breath tickled her shoulder as he whispered the threat into her ear. With his fingertips, he caressed the sensitive flesh of her bare neck, traced the line of her throat down to her chest, and teased the swell of her breasts bound tightly in the bodice of her gown.

"A maiden," he continued, "would never let a strange man take liberties with her in the forest, would she?"

Before she could answer, his supple fingers gripped the bodice of her gown and pulled it down, baring her breasts.

She gasped but didn't blush, even when he stared hungrily at her full breasts, even when he took them into his large strong hands and held them tightly, lifting and molding them against his palms.

"A beautiful lady to be sure," he said, "but no blushing maiden." He rubbed her red and tender nipples with the rough pads of his thumbs. "No matter. I love a lying lady more than a fainting maiden."

"I'm not lying," she said, though her every move proved her a liar. After all, what scared maiden would arch her back and push her breasts into the hands of her captor? He caressed her nipples until they were sore and stiff and aching. Without warning, he pinched them in tandem and she gasped, a rich womanly sound that echoed through the woods. He pinched her nipples again, twisting them gently between his thumb and forefinger.

Mona moaned, as no maiden would.

Malcolm, her Merlin, only chuckled as he teased and tenderly tortured her breasts until they felt heavy in his hands. He took her nipple between his lips and sucked it greedily. It hardened in his hot wet mouth. She arched again in her bonds as he drew on her nipple, pulling it deeper into his mouth and rubbing the very tip of it with his tongue.

He pulled away and met her hooded, heated gaze.

"Still no blushes," he said. Before she could protest, he took her other nipple into his mouth, sucking on it hard enough she groaned. But he was right. Not a blush to be found on any part of her body.

He worked his mouth's magic on her breasts until they throbbed on her chest like twin hearts. He kissed a path from her breasts to her neck and put his mouth to her ear again.

"The two most beautiful breasts I've ever sucked," he said, "and yet not a blush in sight. Let's find out if you're a maiden once and for all."

Malcolm yanked up the skirt of her gown, raising it to her stomach. Then he grasped her thigh, lifted her leg, and draped it over the low yew branch at her hip. He took her other leg and wrapped it over another branch. She wasn't merely tied to the tree now, but spread open on it, hands above her head, thighs forced impossibly wide. Trapped. Bound. Exposed. Who was beguiling whom here?

But perhaps she could still win the game.

Malcolm ran his fingers up her trapped thighs.

"You mustn't," she said, trying desperately to stay in character when she what she wanted to say was, *You must. You absolutely must.*

"But I will," he said. "Let's see if this maiden's cunt has a maidenhead." He cupped her between her thighs, holding her pussy in his palm. The forest was cool that morning, and his fingers were almost cold against her burning flesh. He ran the tip of one finger down the seam of her vulva, splitting the slit and parting her opening. He slowly slid one long cool finger inside her vagina. She shuddered in pleasure at the penetration, shuddered again when a second finger joined it. Slowly he moved his fingers in a wide spiral inside of her, opening her and spreading her, spreading her and opening her wet red inner flesh until her wetness dripped out of her and down his hands.

And if that wasn't torture enough, Malcolm found the tender hollow inside her where she ached to be touched and kneaded it with the calloused tips of his two fingers.

"Soaking wet," he said into her ear, "and hot as the sun, but no maidenhead to be found." He turned his hand inside her and pushed a third finger into her, prying her open even more for him. She wriggled and twisted but couldn't escape his probing touch, not that she wanted to. What a terrible maiden she'd turned out to be.

"You are cruel," she said, pushing her hips into his hand. "You are no gentleman."

"True," he said. "No gentleman would do this to a lost damsel in the woods."

He opened his trousers and took out his cock, thick and long and stiff as iron. He pressed the swollen tip into her open aching hole. With her hips in his hands he lifted her and brought her down onto his cock, impaling her with it.

She cried out in ecstasy, and Malcolm laughed again in her ear.

"The sword Excalibur was never buried so deep in the stone as I am in your cunt," he said. "And still no blushes."

She wanted to protest but was too busy panting to speak. She was speared on his thick cock, split open, her back trapped against the rough bark of the tree as he rammed into her with deep, rough thrusts. Her naked breasts rubbed against the linen of his tunic and his hands held her in a bruising grip. She knew she would look in the mirror tomorrow and see black-and-blue fingerprints all over her ass from how hard he lifted and lowered her onto his cock again and again.

Malcolm grunted as he fucked her, a heady male sound that stoked her own pleasure as it revealed his.

"Not a maid," he said, between panting breaths. "Not even a lady could take this cock like you do. Must be a whore. Must be my whore."

He worked her on his cock, controlling her every movement with his hands until she was nearly screaming from the need to come. She felt his fingers digging even harder into her flesh as he rutted into her. He bounced her on his cock until she thought she might split in half on it. The shaft grazed her swollen clitoris with every thrust, the friction delicious.

Malcolm lifted her again, hitching her up the trunk of the tree to pound into her even harder. She tilted her pelvis to feel more of his cock rubbing and grazing her clitoris. She rocked up and down on his brutal organ until she couldn't hold back another second. With a cry, she came so hard she scared the birds from the upper branches of the yew tree they coupled against. Her orgasm came in wave after wave of sharp contractions so racking she knew Malcolm could feel them. He rasped a low "fuck" into her ear.

As her climax waned, Malcolm pounded his into her. Mona forced herself to concentrate, to keep her eyes on the prize, the book of magic in his cloak and the answers it held. She went limp against the tree and let Malcolm use her body. His head fell back as he pumped his last thrusts into her. That was the moment Mona slipped one hand out of the scarf still knotted loosely around her wrist. His hips bucked up and into her, and when he let out that low grunt that signaled he was coming inside her, she slipped her other hand out of the other loop around her wrist.

At the height of ecstasy when his dark eyes were shut tight and his face wore a mask of pleasure so intense it looked like pain, Mona shoved him backward. He fell into the hawthorn bush where he was immediately caught by the thorny vines.

He struggled a moment before going limp, looking up at her, and laughing.

"I knew it—she *is* a witch," he said. He struggled again, wincing as the thorns tore at his clothes.

Mona unwrapped her legs from the tree branches.

"I suppose you're right," she said as she fixed her mussed hair and retied her gown's bodice. "But a good witch, yes?"

"I don't know about that," he said, "but you were certainly an enjoyable witch. Come and let me enjoy you again."

His cock was already getting hard a second time. She crossed her arms over her chest and looked down at him with an eyebrow raised.

"You're the only man I know who would get hard while trapped in a hawthorn bush," she said as she walked to his cloak, still hanging on the end of the tree branch. His warm seed spilled down her thighs as she walked.

"Your cunt must have bewitched me," he said. "Come

bewitch it again." He lifted his hips in invitation, an invitation she ignored.

She found the leather-bound book of magic in his cloak pocket.

"I wonder if this how the Lady of the Lake got Merlin," Mona said. "She let him fuck her and then when he was coming, she pushed him into the shrubs."

"Probably so," Malcolm said. "The painting only captures one frame of the story. It never tells the whole tale. And the painting doesn't reveal what the Lady of the Lake found in Merlin's book of magic either."

"Let's find out…" Mona said as she pulled the book from its pocket. It was a beautiful book, bound in rich dark leather, weathered and faded and soft to the touch. She pressed open the pages to the center and found an elaborate pen-and-ink drawing of a man and woman having sex against the trunk of a tree. Mona turned a page and found another pen and ink drawing of a man and woman having sex on the ground. She flipped page after page and saw nothing but pictures of couples coupling in every possible position.

It wasn't a book of magic. It was pornography.

Meanwhile Malcolm, still trapped in the hawthorn bush, laughed again, laughed at her.

"You," she said, turning on him. "You said if I got your book, I'd know how you did all this."

"I said, if you'll recall, that if you could steal my book, you'd know how I did my tricks. I never said my magic tricks. I have more than one kind of trick."

"You wicked wizard," she said and threw the book at him. It landed on his stomach in a flurry of pages.

"You almost hit my cock," he said. "You are a witch."

"I am and this witch is going to leave you there," she said.

"You wouldn't dare." He narrowed his eyes at her, suspicious.

"You deserve it," Mona said.

"I gave you an orgasm so strong it nearly snapped my prick off, and you're saying I deserve being stuck in a fucking demonic shrub for playing one little trick on you?"

"Fine," she said. "I'll let you out. But only this once." She tiptoed into the bush and carefully began to extract Malcolm's clothes from the thorny vines of the bush.

"Mona, darling," Malcolm said as she pulled a thorn from his tunic. "I have to tell you something."

"Yes?"

Without warning the vines of the hawthorn wrapped around Mona's stomach and pulled her to the ground. She struggled but couldn't free herself. She was trapped on her back, bound by living magic vines. They had her by the wrists, by the ankles, by the stomach…

"Malcolm," she growled.

He straddled her stomach. "I have many, many tricks…"

Even if Mona wanted to move, she couldn't. The thorny vines had her and the littlest movement would mean the thorns would snare her skin. She had to lie perfectly still as Malcolm dragged her gown to her hips. More vines wrapped around her legs and pulled her thighs wide open. She panted as Malcolm found her clitoris with his fingertips and stroked it until it swelled. And once it was swollen and throbbing, he dipped his head and licked it. Then he pushed three fingers inside her wet cunt and into that tender hollow again, kneading it while he sucked that throbbing knot with such masterful precision Mona could have cried from the incredible pleasure. When she was as close to climax as she could get without coming, Malcolm drew his fingers out of her. His cock was stiff again, red and dripping as he mounted her. He thrust into her, slowly and hard as Mona lay there, unmoving but for the rise and fall of her breasts with her every heavy breath.

Malcolm pushed the bodice of her gown down again. He ran his hands over her breasts as he moved inside her.

"This is my magic," he said softly as he caressed her nipples with his fingertips, caressed and tugged them, tugged and teased them. His dark, wavy hair fell over his dark, wild eyes. "Making you ache. Making you wet. Making you pant and moan for me. Making you come and come again. Does it really matter how I do it as long as I do it?"

"No," she said as she lifted her hips a centimeter off the hard ground. A thorn bit into her belly but it was worth it for the jolt of pleasure she felt when Malcolm's cock shifted inside her.

"Good, because a magician never reveals his secrets."

He kissed her lips as he rode her, gently at first, then harder—short, sharp thrusts into her needy cunt. Mona wanted to move, had to move, but couldn't move because of the thorny vines holding her in place. The tension was sweet at first, being fucked while she couldn't move a muscle, but soon it grew too potent to bear. Her eyes ran with tears and her hips and stomach tightened, her fingernails dug deep into the green earth below her, the only movement she could make without being scratched by the thorns. Her breaths came in quick bursts as Malcolm speared her over and over until she was shaken by a fierce orgasm, a thousand wicked spasms deep inside of her. Malcolm cried out as he orgasmed again, filling her up with spurt after spurt of his hot semen.

"I'm a terrible Lady of the Lake," Mona said as she went limp and sated underneath him. "I was supposed to beguile you, Merlin. Instead you beguiled me."

"Shall I beguile you a third time?" he asked.

"Beguile me forever," she said as he started to move inside her again.

Mona forgot all about his secrets, his powers, his magic. The vines tightened on her wrists and thighs. She smiled at the pinprick of pain. His kissed her and she trembled with longing, with pleasure, with love.

This was the only magic Mona needed.

———

ABOUT THE AUTHOR

Tiffany Reisz is the *USA Today* bestselling author of the Romance Writers of America RITA®-winning Original Sinners series from Harlequin's Mira Books.

Her erotic fantasy *The Red*—the first entry in the Godwicks series, self-published under the banner 8th Circle Press—was named an NPR Best Book of the Year and a Goodreads Best Romance of the Month.

Tiffany lives in Kentucky with her husband, author Andrew Shaffer, and two cats. The cats are not writers.

Subscribe to the Tiffany Reisz email newsletter:

www.tiffanyreisz.com/mailing-list